The Unnamed Press
P.O. Box 411272
Los Angeles CA 90041

Published in North America by The Unnamed Press

1 3 5 7 9 10 8 6 4 2

Copyright © 2018 by Stefan G. Bucher

ISBN 978-1-944700-492

Library of Congress Control Number: 2017946989
This book is distributed by Publishers Group West
Designed by Stefan G. Bucher for 344 Design LLC
Printed and bound in China

This book is a work of fiction. Names, characters, places, and incidents are wholly fictional or are used fictitiously. Any resemblance to actual events or persons, living or dead, is entirely coincidental.

All rights reserved, including the right to reproduce this book or portions thereof in any form whatsoever. Permissions inquiries may be directed to info@unnamedpress.com

LOVE LETTERS

1 **When was the last time you thought about letters?** They're among the first things our parents teach us, and once we've learned how to understand and employ them, we never forget. We use them every day — to read, to write — but we become so good at using them that we give the individual characters no more thought than Mozart might have given a passing C-sharp note. How often does a fish pause to consider the water?

2 Letters are bits of code, little graphic symbols, glyphs that stand for sounds — sounds that combine into words that come together to form thoughts. They let us show what's in our heads to others — even to people thousands of miles and hundreds of years away — and see what they think about our ideas. Those people can then build on our thoughts and come up with their own. Do that with a few hundred million people for a few thousand years and you've got yourself a culture! All because of letters.

3 Without letters we wouldn't have Shakespeare, we wouldn't have the Beatles, and we wouldn't have that comment you posted online earlier today. Without letters we wouldn't have science. Passing on information by word of mouth might get you to the next village, but it won't get you to Mars.

4 As a graphic designer, I spend a ridiculous amount of time thinking about letters. I shape them into logotypes and movie titles; I arrange them by the millions to make books and posters. I love letters. Always have. I started copying the big, bold cartoon letterforms from comic books when I was three years old. I've always known that letters have personality. Usually, it expresses itself in elegant curves and decisive corners, in size and color, in the way the letters play with one another. But I thought it was high time to take a different look at the alphabet — to let each letter truly come to life in its own right.

5 For this book, I stuck to the basic Roman alphabet. Of course, not every *X* or *G* or *W* looks the same. These letters are simply the ones that presented themselves to me. You'll come across wildly different characters once you start paying individual attention to them. Some are young, some are old. Heck, some of them may be *italic*. Who am I to judge? Like us, they come in all shapes and sizes. As with humans, there is no right or wrong way for a letter to be.

6 Please enjoy spending time with the LetterHeads! I hope it will make you take note of the letters you use every day and appreciate how hard they work for you! After years of letters helping me express what's going on in my head, this book is about them and how they're feeling. → Stefan G. Bucher

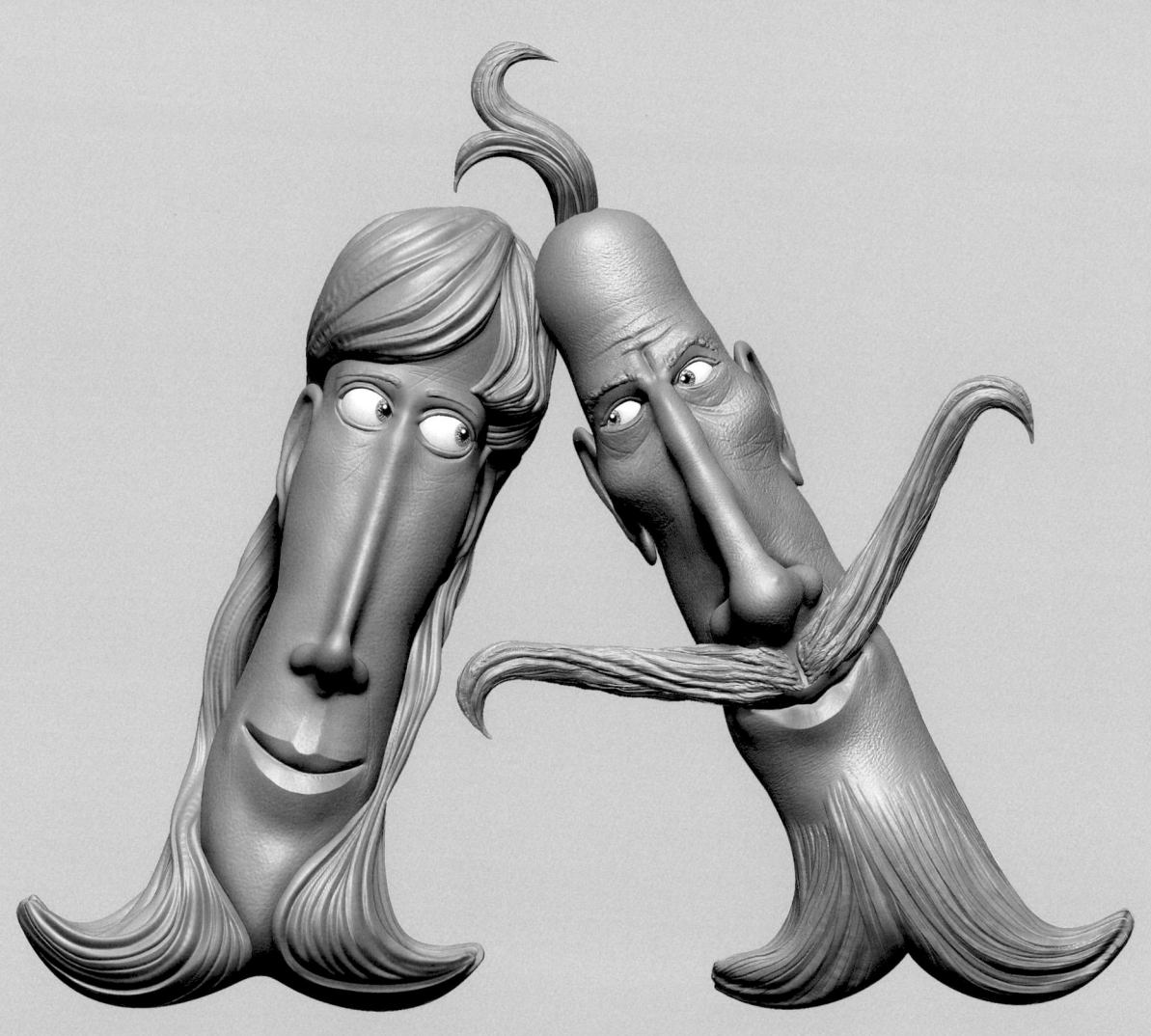

Abigail adores Álvaro's Andalusian accent.

Abigail adores Álvaro's Andalusian accent.

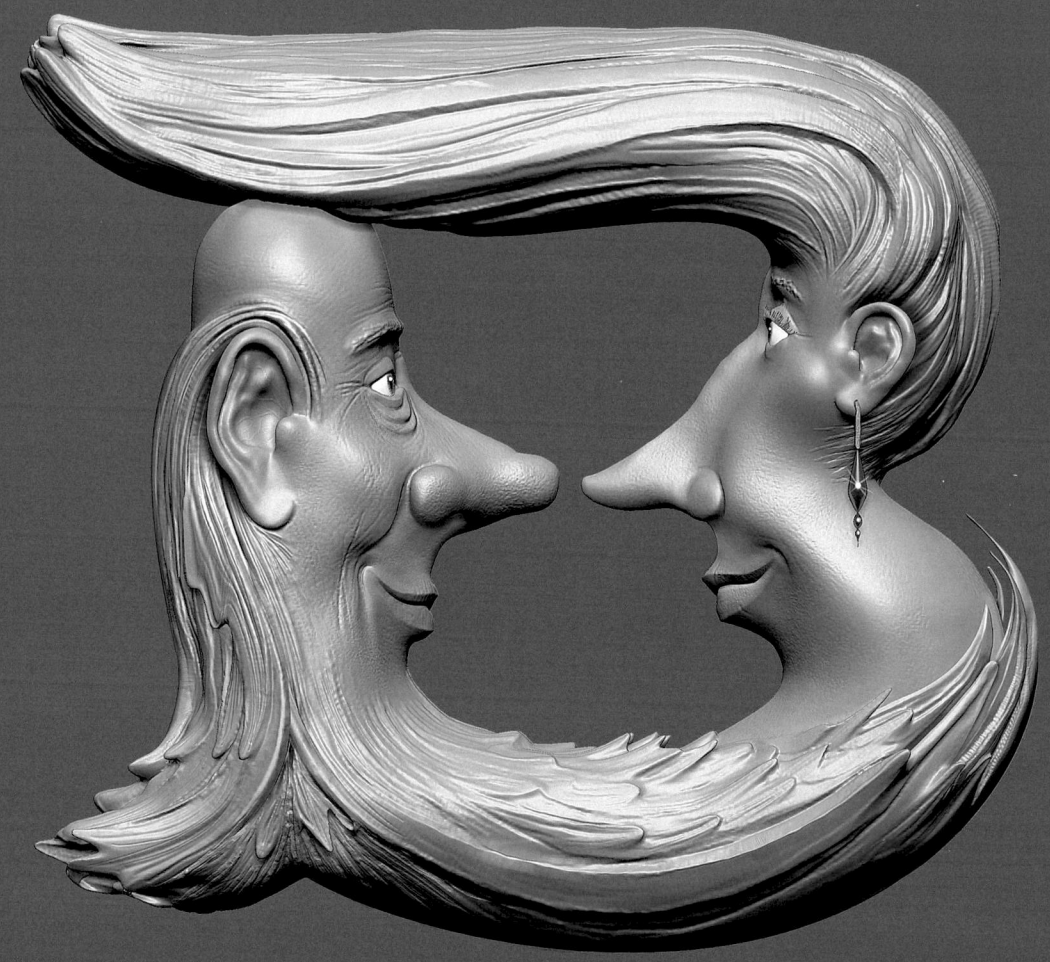

Bertram and Beatrice are besotted.

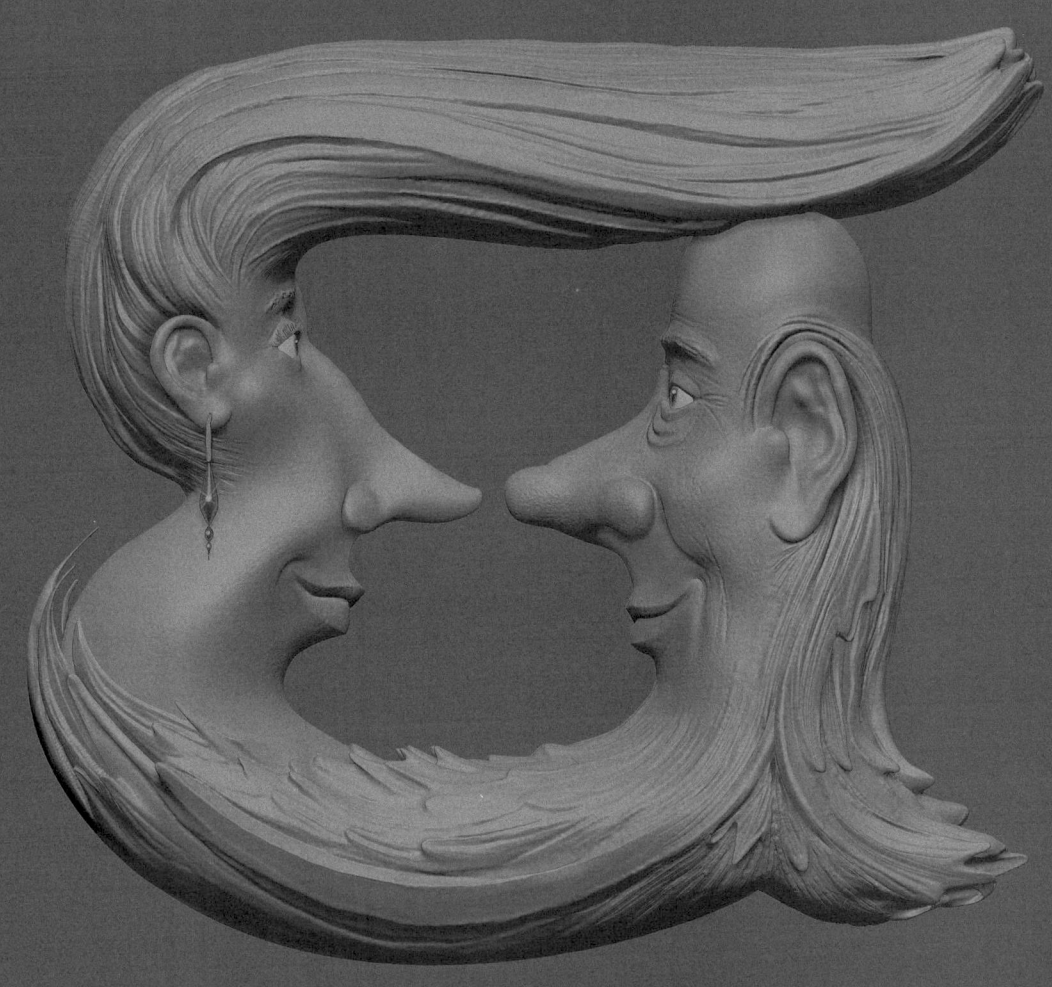

Bertram and Beatrice are besotted.

Cecil considers chivalry critical.

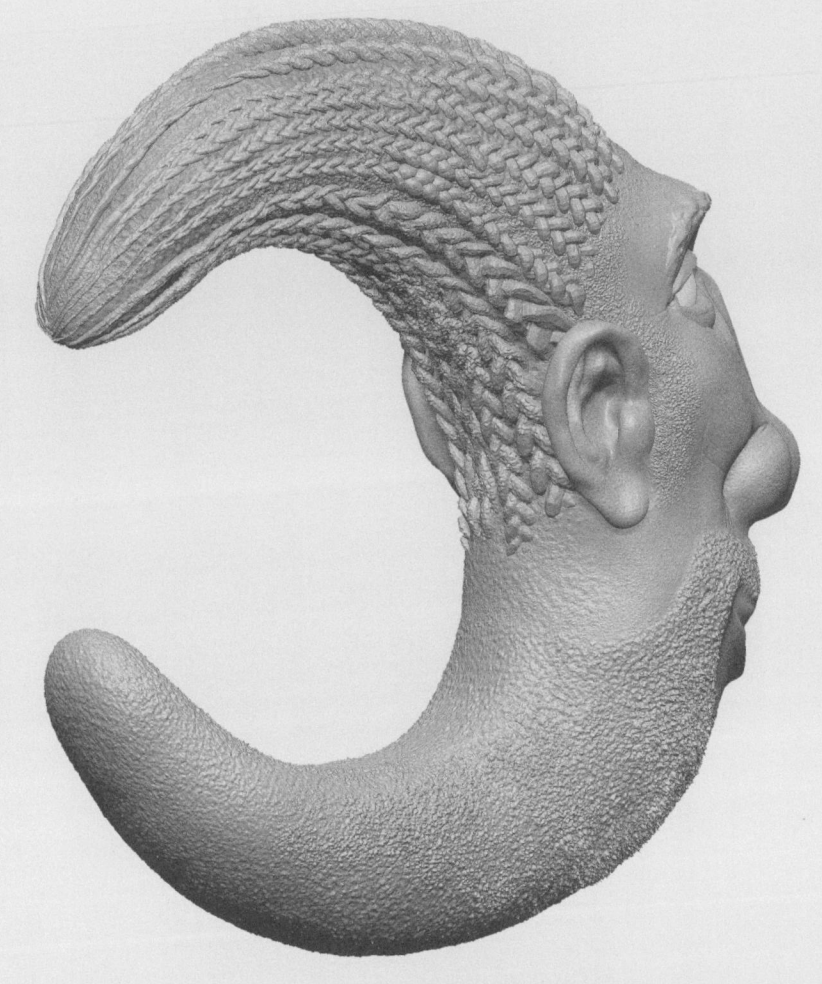

Cecil considers chivalry critical.

Deedra is dreaming of Doyald.

Deedra is dreaming of Doyald.

Eiko is all ears.

Eiko is all ears.

François is famously fastidious.

François is famously fastidious.

Guillermo is glad whenever Gaétan glides in with gossip.

Guillermo is glad whenever Gaétan glides in with gossip.

Harold's heart holds only Hector.

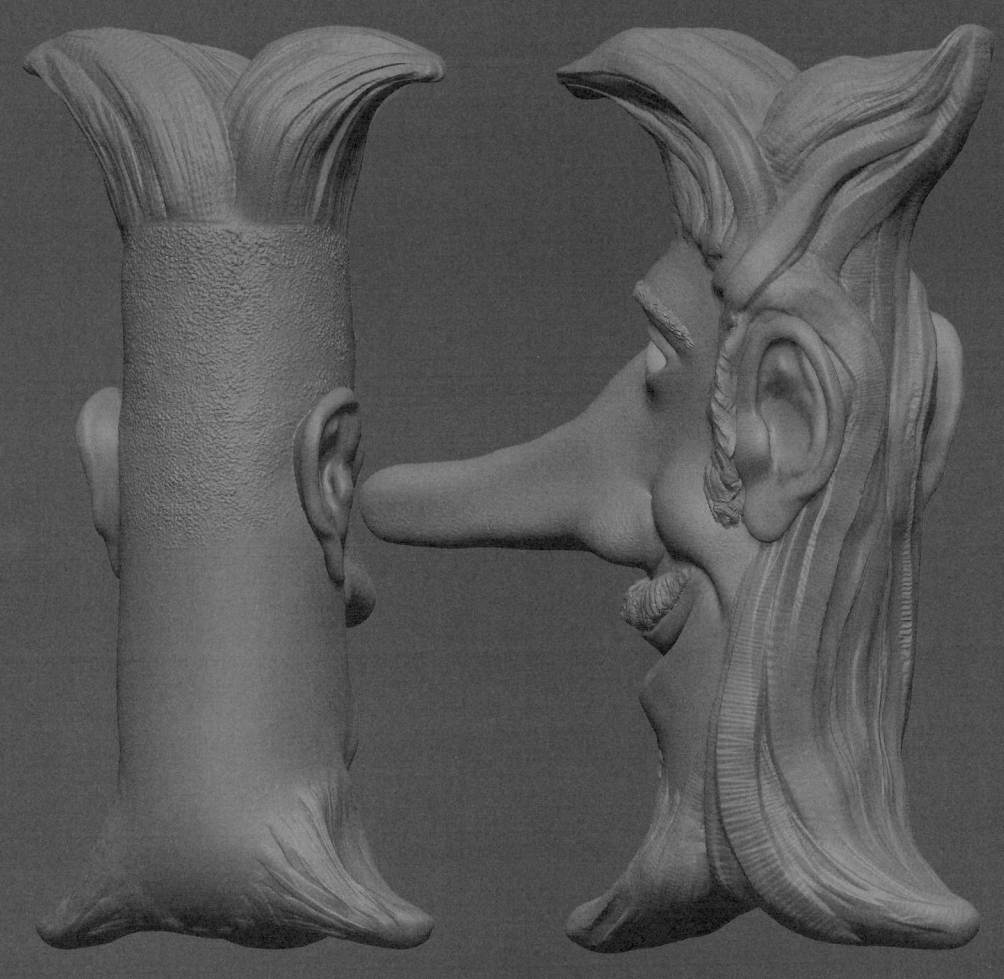

Harold's heart holds only Hector.

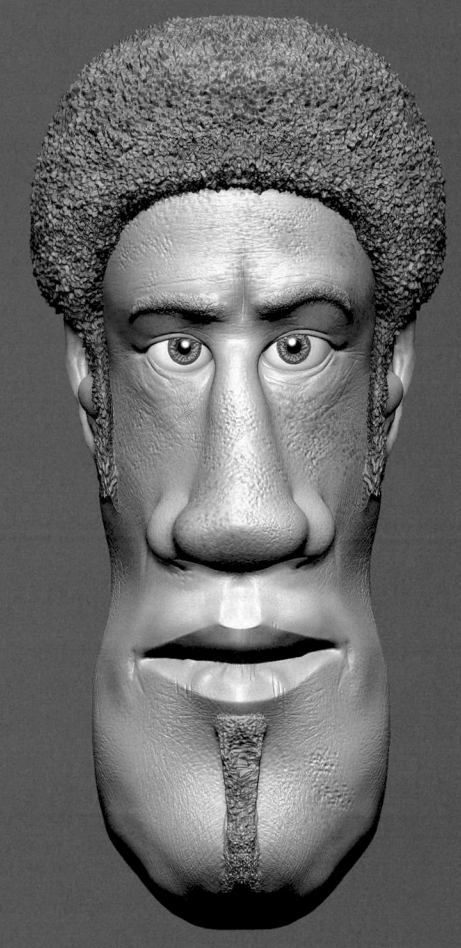

Ingmar is imperturbable.

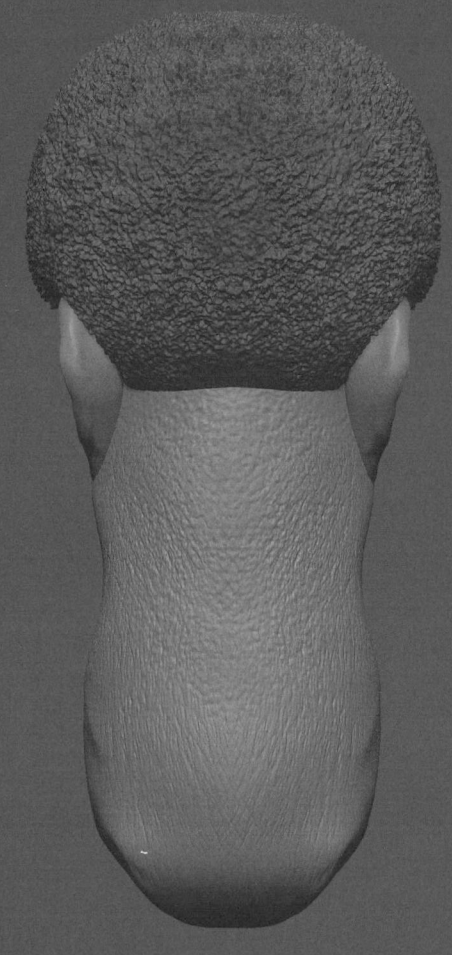

ingmar is imperturbable.

Julius is feeling jinxed.

Julius is feeling jinxed.

Klaus has gone off-kilter.

Klaus has gone off-kilter.

Lilian loves Leah's languid ways.

Lilian loves Leah's languid ways.

Myrna and Myrtle mustn't move!

Myrna and Myrtle mustn't move!

It's nothing but negativity with Neville and Nuri.

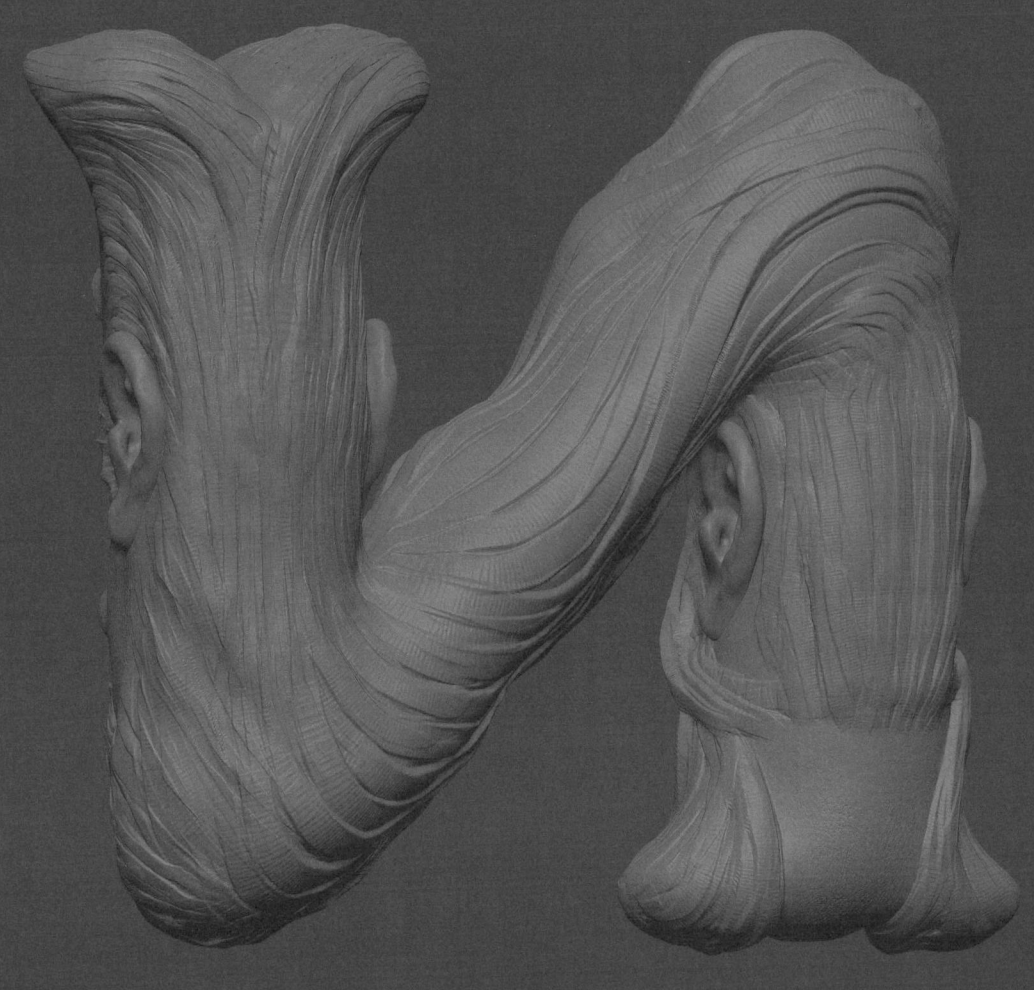

It's nothing but negativity with Neville and Nun.

Ophelia is overjoyed!

Percival perceives perfume as putrid.

Percival perceives perfume as putrid.

Qasim can't keep quiet!

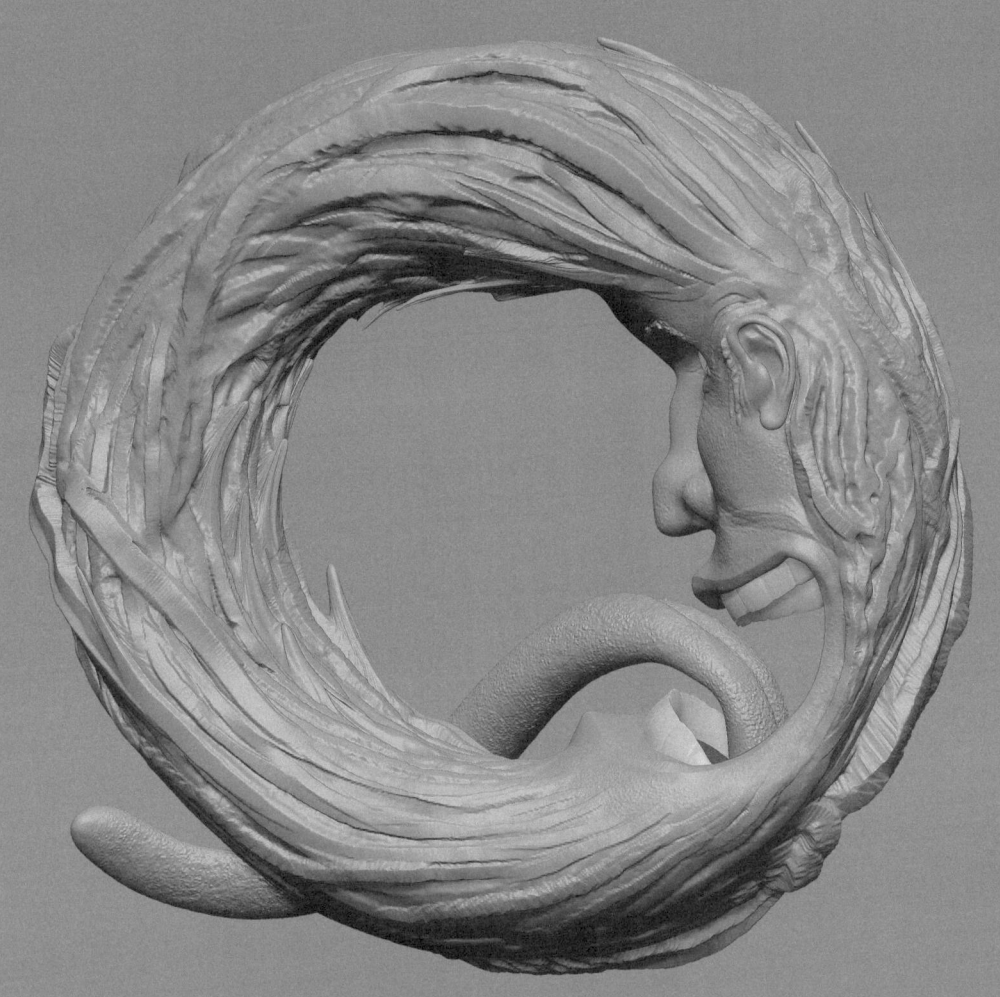

Qasim can't keep quiet!

Ragnar and RaeQuan are reticent realists.

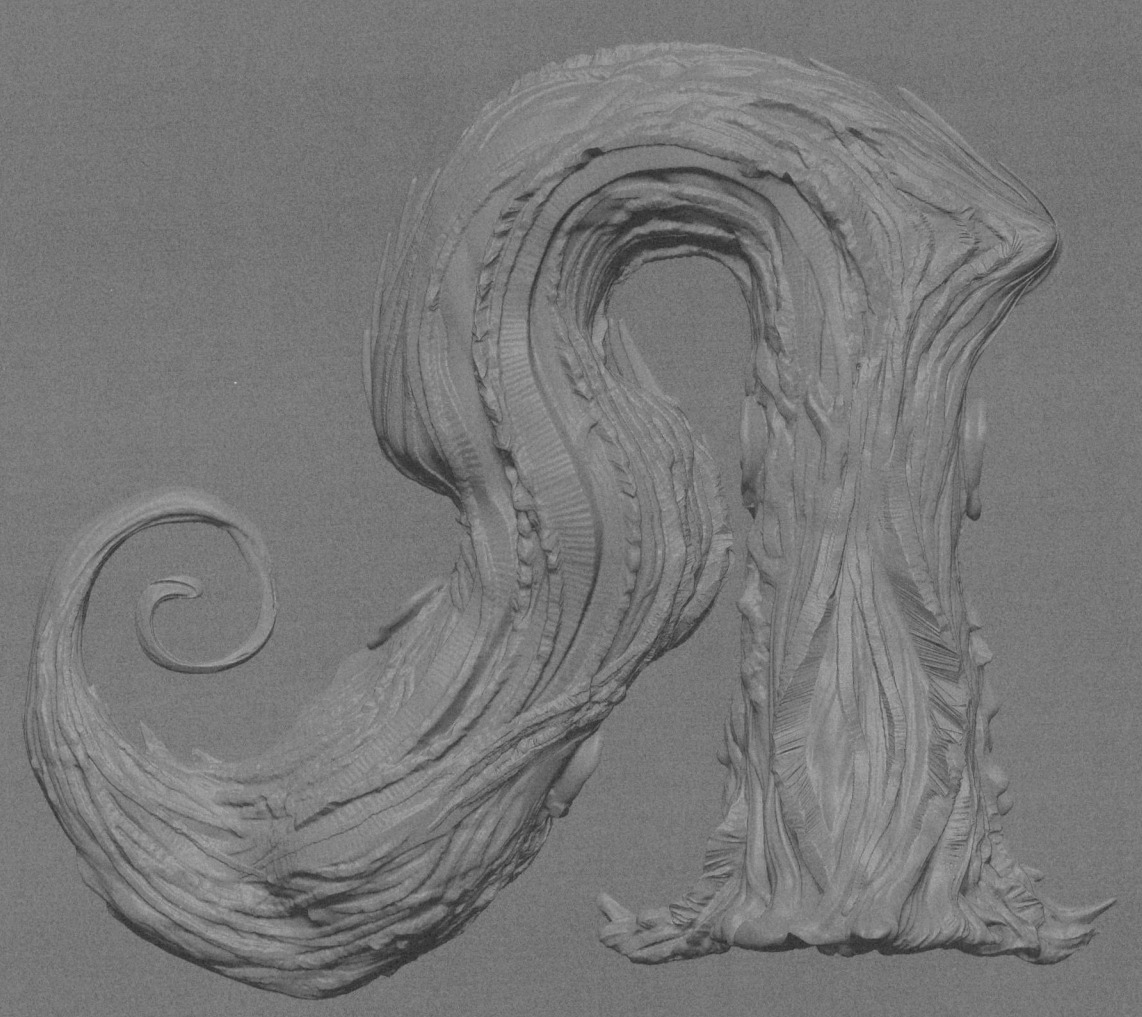

Ragnar and RaeQuan are reticent realists.

Siona is searching for shooting stars.

Siona is searching for shooting stars.

Torvald is toilworn from telling tall tales.

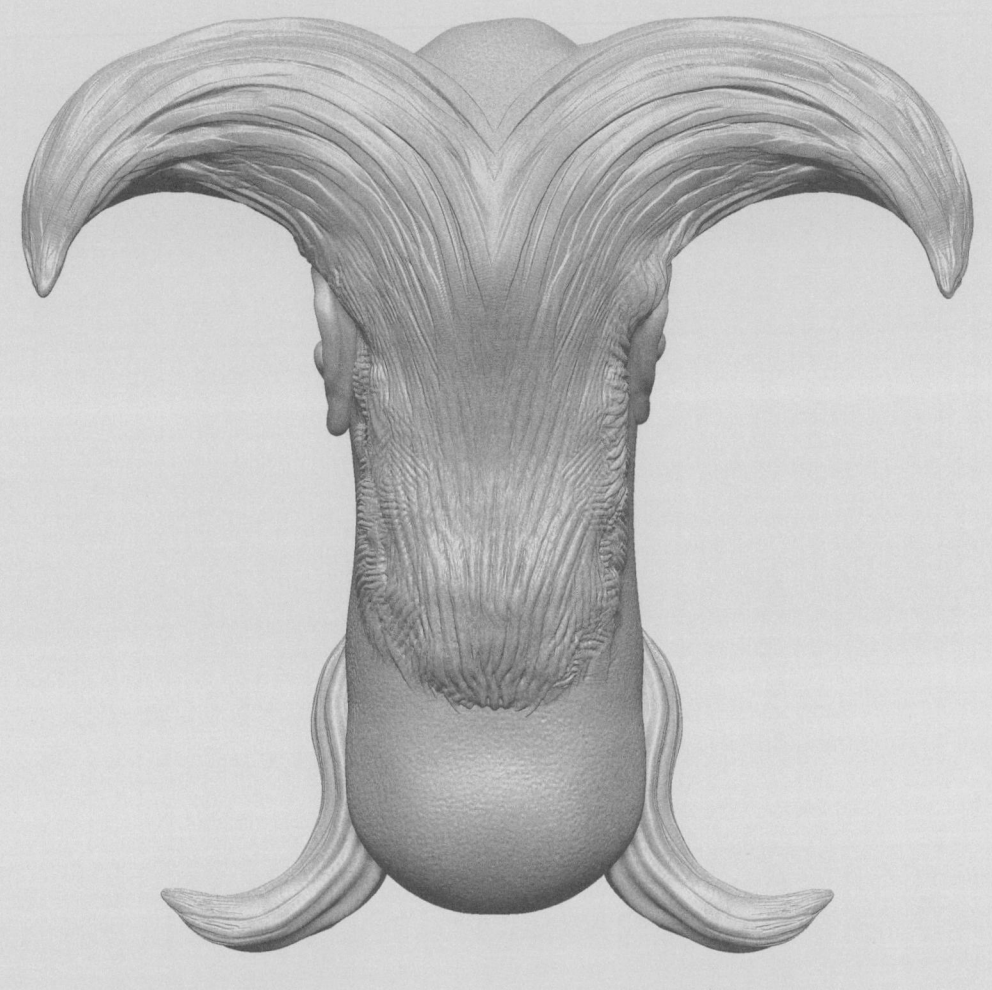

Torvald is toilworn from telling tall tales.

Ulysses and Umberto understand unlimess.

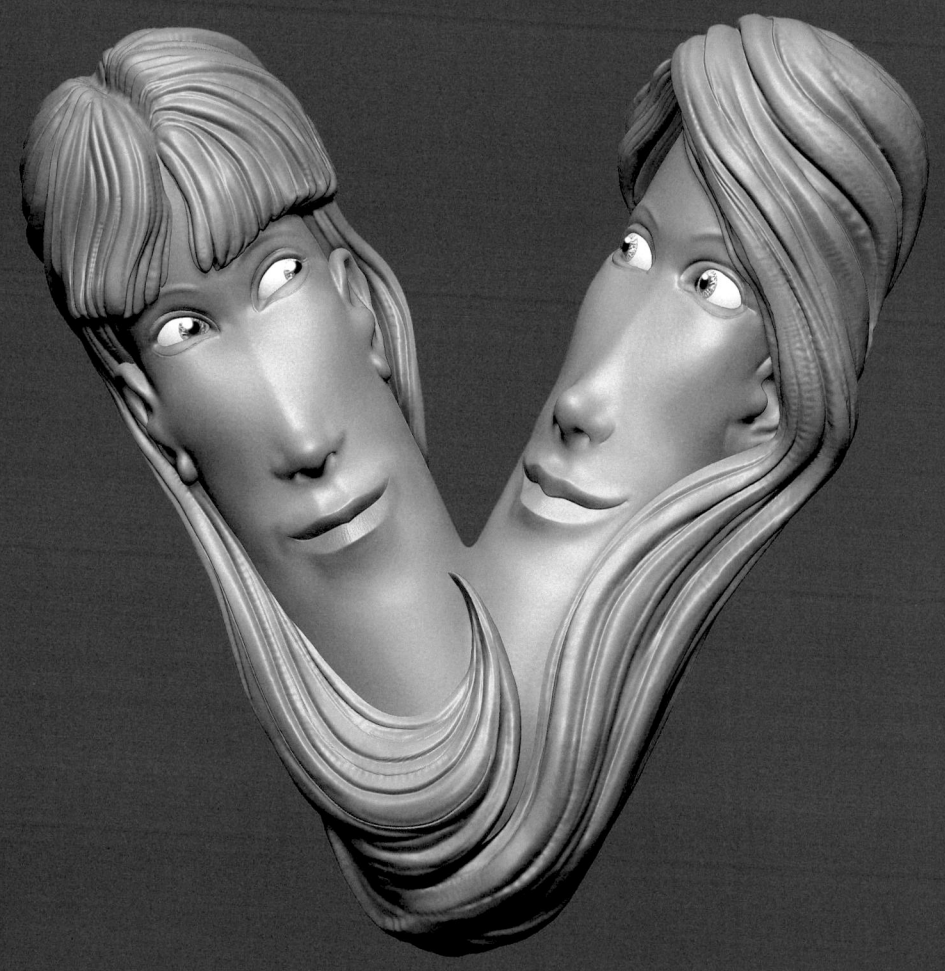

Velma and Vanja value each other's vivacity.

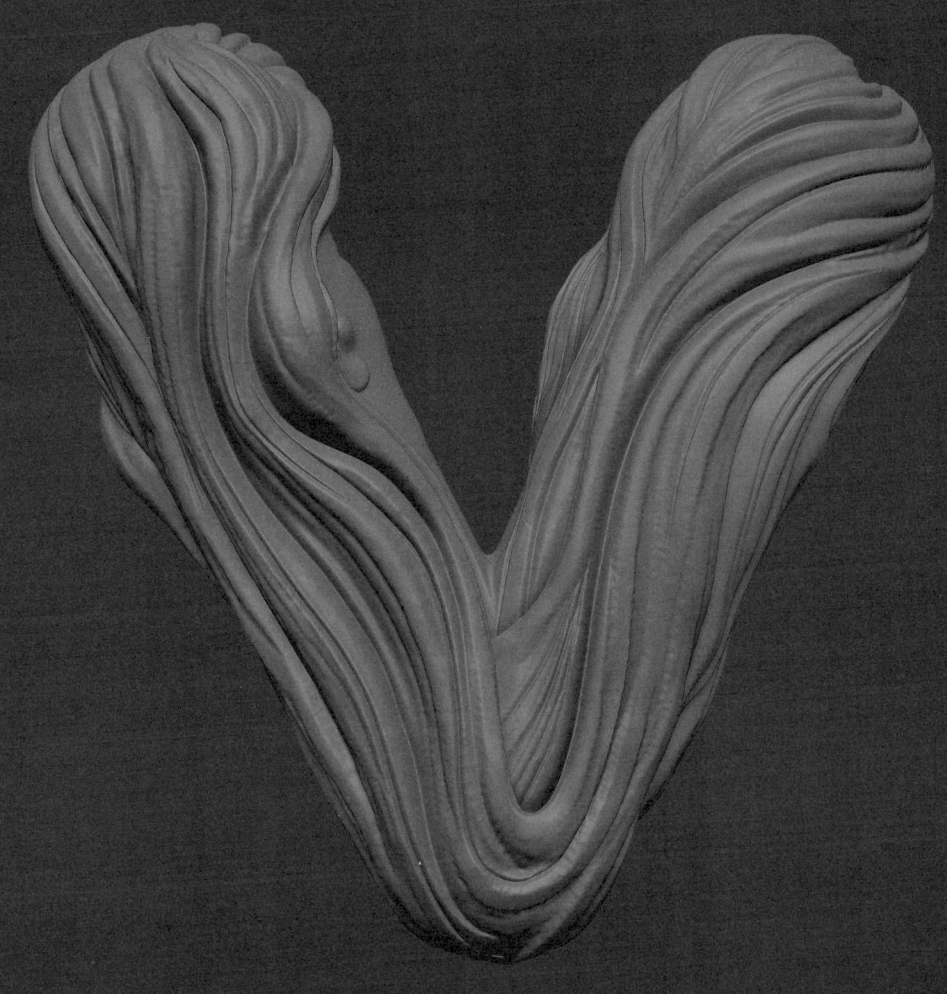

Velma and Vanja value each other's vivacity.

Wadi'ah wishes that Wanda and Wendy weren't warring.

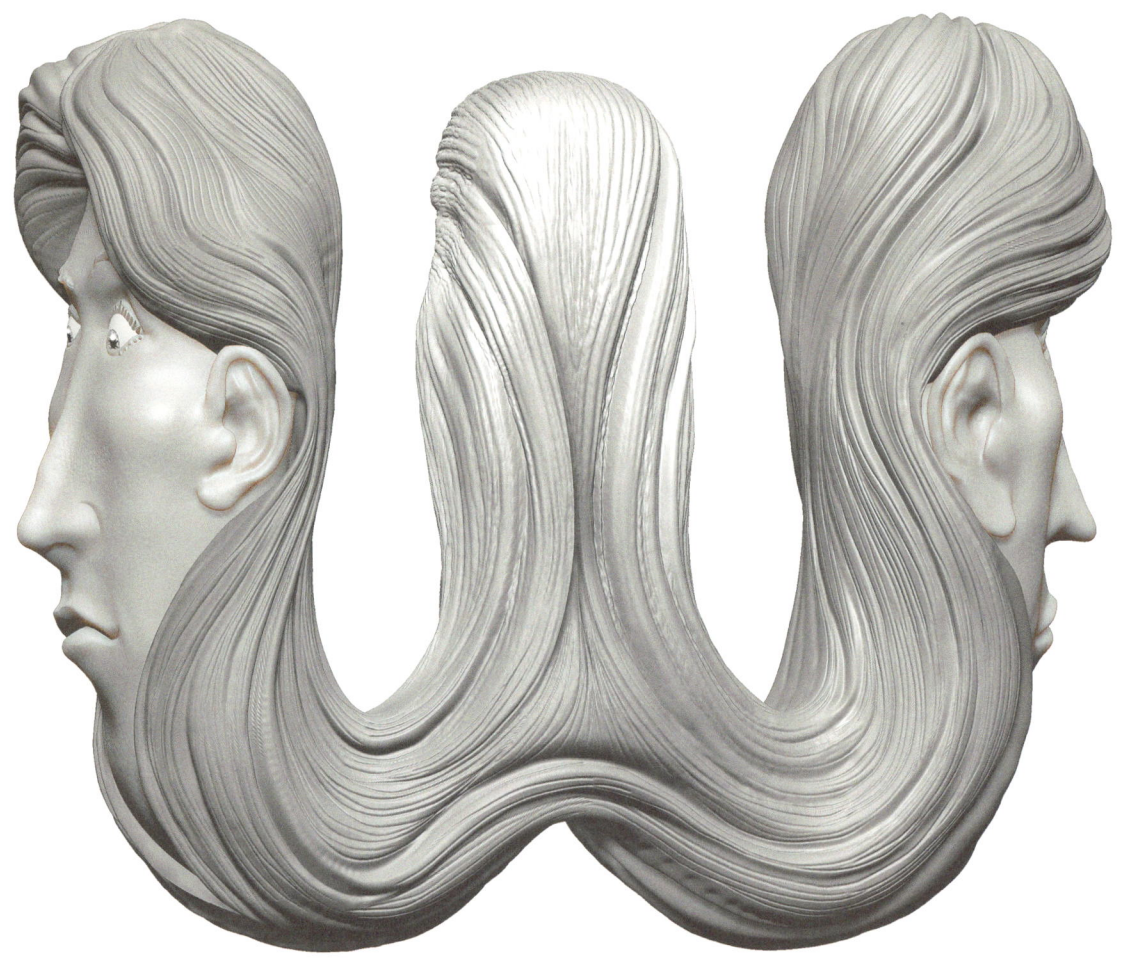

Wadi'ah wishes that Wanda and Wendy weren't warring.

Xuanxing is having an extracorporeal experience.

Xuanxing is having an extracorporeal experience.

Yisador and Yevgeny yearn for yesterday.

Yisrador and Yevgeny yearn for yesterday.

Zebadiah is zealously un-zany.

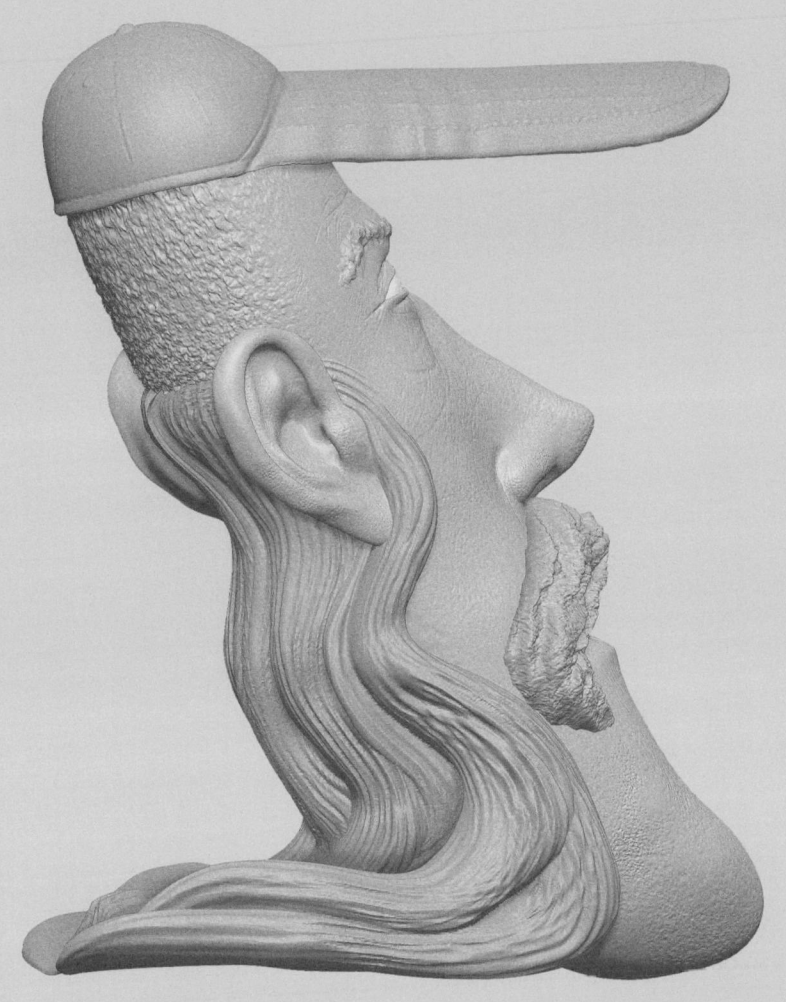

Zebadiah is zealously un-zany.

A FEW NOTES on the background colors *(and a few bonus notes on where some of the characters got their names)*

Abigail and Álvaro's favorite color is an alluring apple green.

Also mine.

Guillermo goes gaga for gold.

Guillermo is named for Guillermo del Toro, who creates beautiful monsters. I wish Gaétan were my pet raven.

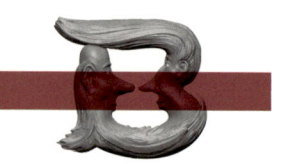

Bertram and Beatrice love light burgundy.

Perhaps they also love a light burgundy, but in the absence of hands to lift a glass… perhaps they bribe their waiter to bring them straws?

Harold is hot for heliotrope. Hector hates it.

Harold is named after Harold Ramis and after my friend Aron's poodle, who is named after Harold Lloyd. Hector is named Hector because he's hectoring Harold.

Cecil's favorite color lies somewhere between cyan and celadon.

It's not pronounced CE-cil. It's CEE-cil. He's a C.

Ingmar insists on indigo.

Ingmar is named for director Ingmar Bergman, just because.

Deedra delights in daffodil.

Doyald is my dear friend Doyald Young, who was a brilliant letterform designer and a wonderful man. "Deedra" means "sorrowful" or "heartbroken."

Julius gets some joy from jade.

The first Julius I ever knew was my elementary school music teacher, Herr Julius. He made me sad. Then again, the way he taught music kept me focused on the visual arts.

Eiko is excited about ecru.

Eiko is named for Eiko Ishioka, an extraordinary graphic designer who also designed the costumes for Tarsem's first four movies.

Klaus kinda likes khaki.

Klaus is named for Klaus Voormann, who designed the Beatles' Revolver cover, which has driven me mad with envy for many, many years.

François favors fuchsia.

I fear that François and I share a view of the world more often than I'd like.

Lilian loves lemon yellow.

The name Lilian comes from the lily flower. It symbolizes innocence and beauty. Leah is an homage to Leah Hoffmitz, my first and most important type and lettering teacher.

Mustard isn't Myrna and Myrtle's favorite color, but they make do.

My friend Jane and I decided years ago that "myrna" would be our new word for "nerdy cool." Myrtle seemed like a suitable companion name.

Torvald is tickled by turquoise.

Torvald is named after the Thorvald family in my friend J. Ryan Stradal's book "Kitchens of the Great Midwest." I dropped the h.

Neville and Nuri barely agree on navy blue as nonoffensive.

Nuri is a Hebrew name that means "glaring flame." Neville is named for Neville Page, who introduced me to digital sculpting.

Ulysses and Umberto agree that ultramarine is unbeatable.

Umberto is named after Umberto Eco and Ulysses after Ulysses S. Grant III, who also makes a cameo in my book The Yeti Story.

Ophelia is obsessed with orange.

Ophelia makes the face I make when I get my hands on some really good chocolate.

Velma and Vanja venerate violet.

Velma is an homage to Velma Dinkley from Scooby-Doo. Vanja is a female name in Scandinavia and Bulgaria, but a male name in Russia, where it's spelled with a y.

Percival is about to turn puce.

I have a lousy sense of smell. Looking at Percival and his struggles, I think I got lucky.

If only Wanda and Wendy would wave a white flag.

Wadi'ah is an Urdu name meaning "calm" or "peaceable." Wanda and Wendy are a reference to the movie A Fish Called Wanda.

Qasim is unquestionably into quicksilver.

Qasim is an Arabic name that means "one who divides goods among his people."

Xuanxing can't explain his attraction to the color xanth.

In Chinese, "xuan" means "mysterious," and "xing" means "form." Xuanxing is a mysterious character. My friend Dominik Wei-Fieg came up with his name.

Ragnar and RaeQuan recommend a robust rust color.

Ragnar is a Norse name meaning "warrior from the gods." RaeQuan is such a rare name that I couldn't find its meaning, but I really like the sound of it!

Yevgeny thinks yellow is yucky. Yisador... yeah, he likes it.

Yevgeny is named for author Yevgeny Zamyatin, Yisador is an alternate spelling of Isidor, or Izzy to his friends. It's also a nod to dancer Isadora Duncan.

Siona is seduced by salmon.

Siona is a Hindi name that means "stars."

Zebadiah thinks the color zomp is zesty.

Zomp, like xanth, is an actual color. It's popular in Australia and New Zealand.

STEFAN G. BUCHER'S

Letter Heads

AN ECCENTRIC ALPHABET

Dedicated to all the Charlies

FURWORD
by Patricia Field, Charlie's Fairy Godmother

Lara called me when she met Charlie in the lobby of a hotel and asked for my opinion on rescuing him, to which I replied with no hesitation, "Get the dog."

It was the best decision she ever made.

INSPIRATION

Charlie the Pomeranian dreams of a world where hotels and doorman buildings open their lobbies and join paws with local shelters to foster animals and get more involved with adoption events to help his fellow furry friends find homes just like him. Head to prettyconnected.com/charlie to learn more!

Based on the true story of Charlie King, a senior Pomeranian rescued from the lobby of a hotel through their pet adoption program.

Hi, I'm Charlie. I live in the lobby of the Pom Springs Hotel.

I get to be the hotel's tour guide and show guests all around the property. They just ask for me at the front desk, and I'm at their service.

I like it here. I get to meet new families every day in hopes that one of them will adopt me. Then, I'll have my very own family! Ms. Jane at the front desk says it will happen soon, but I don't know when that will be.

"Charlie, can you show Grace and her mom to the pool?" asks Ms. Jane.

"Sure! Come with me."

"I can introduce you to my friends along the way! To get to the pool, we go through the door, past the waterfall, and over the bridge. Say hi to the fish!"

"Just before we get to the pool is the home of my turtle and rabbit friends!" I explain. "Everyone, meet Grace and her mom! They're staying with us for the weekend."

"Do you all live together?" asks Grace.

"Yes, we're a family!" Scooter, the turtle, replies.

"But you're turtles and rabbits!" exclaims Grace.

"Yes. There are all types of families, and we've decided to make our home together," declares Bella, the rabbit.

"Charlie, where's your family?" Grace asks.

"I don't have one yet, but I'm hoping to find my forever family soon!"

"Then, who tucks you in at night?"
Grace wonders.

I shrug sadly. "Here we are. This is the pool."

"Thank you, Charlie!" Grace and her mom wave goodbye.

As they walk away, I look through the pool gate at all the families and think, *Are you my forever family? Are you!?*

At the front desk, Ms. Jane is helping another family. "Hey, Charlie. Do you mind showing Lucas and his dad to the golf course?"

"Sure, Ms. Jane!"

"Come with me. We can take the golf cart. To get to the golf course, we follow the path straight down past the lake. We'll be there in a jiff."

As we pass the lake, we see the swans coming out from their afternoon swim alongside the ducks and their ducklings.

"Hi, Charlie. Who are your new friends?" asks Maia, the little duckling.

"This is Lucas and his dad. I'm taking them to their golf lesson."

"Is this your family?" asks Lucas.

"Yes, we all live together," answers Mario, the swan.

"But you're swans and duckies!" exclaims Lucas.

"Yes. There are all types of families, biological and adopted, and we've decided to join ours together," Desi, the duck, explains.

"Charlie, where's your family?" asks Lucas.

I smile bravely. "I don't have one yet, but I'm hoping to find my forever family soon!"

"Then, who tucks you in at night?" Lucas wonders.

I shrug sadly. "The golf course is right up here. Have a nice lesson!"

"Thank you, Charlie, for your help." Lucas and his dad wave goodbye.

Feeling a little down, I decide to walk back to the hotel lobby. On my way, I take a break under my favorite willow tree. I'm so deep in thought that I don't even hear George, the night heron, swoop over me.

"What's the matter, Charlie?" asks George.

"Oh, hi, George! I was just thinking about my forever family. Ms. Jane at the front desk says I'll meet them soon, but I don't know when that will be."

"Don't worry, Charlie. When the time is right, it will happen. Until then, you have great friends, and we're your family."

"You're right, George. I feel a lot better. Thank you for listening. I have to get back to the lobby, but I'll see you soon."

As I get ready for bed, just like every night before, I dream my forever family will find me soon.

"Don't worry, Charlie," says Ms. Jane. "We've helped a lot of doggies just like you find their forever family! When you meet them, you'll know. It will happen soon."

The next day, a nice couple from New York arrives. Their names are Lara and James King.

"Now who might you be?" asks Lara softly.

"That's Charlie," answers Ms. Jane. "He's up for adoption. He can show you around while we get your room ready."

"Come with me! I'll introduce you to my friends," I offer. "There's Scooter, Bella, Billy, Desi, and Mario… Oh, and the bees! You have to meet the bees during your stay. They live by the restaurant and make all the honey for the hotel."

Once we return to the lobby after our walk, Ms. Jane says, "Mr. King, your room is ready."

Lara turns to me and smiles. "It was nice to meet you, Charlie. I'll come visit you every day."

And she does. We go for walks and play in the grass. Lara even reads to me in her hotel room, which makes me feel so special!

On their final evening before heading back to New York, Lara and James walk through the lobby on their way to dinner.

"We're going to the restaurant if you'd like to join us, Charlie," offers James.

"Don't worry," Lara assures Ms. Jane. "We'll be sure to get him back before his bedtime and tuck Charlie in."

Tuck me in? I think to myself. *Dinner with a family? Oh, wow. This is going to be the best night ever!*

At the restaurant, Lara lifts me onto her lap and reads me the doggie menu.

"Can I have the canine casserole and a honey-sweet treat for dessert!?" I request excitedly.

James laughs. "Someone has quite the appetite."

Once we're back in the lobby, Lara tucks me in. "I'm going to miss you," she says softly. "Sweet dreams."

James turns to Ms. Jane and asks in a low voice, "Has Charlie been adopted yet?" She shakes her head no.

The next morning, James and Lara pack up the car to head to the airport.

Once they finish loading, James turns to Lara and asks, "All set?"

"There's just one more thing…" Lara says.

She dashes over to Charlie and his animal friends and asks…

"Charlie, do you want to be a part of our forever family?"

My eyes get big, and I feel my tail wagging like crazy.

"YES!!!! Friends, I'm going to New York!"

"Yay, Charlie!" his animal friends cheer. "You finally found your forever family!"